THE SECRET WORLD OF

Falcons

THE SECRET WORLD OF

Falcons

Jill Bailey

RAINTREE
STECK-VAUGHN
PUBLISHERS

A Harcourt Company

Austin   New York
www.raintreesteckvaughn.com

Published by Raintree Steck-Vaughn Publishers, an imprint of Steck-Vaughn Company

Acknowledgments
Project Editors: Sean Dolan and Rebecca Hunter
Production Director: Richard Johnson
Illustrated by Stuart Lafford
Designed by Ian Winton

Planned and produced by Discovery Books

Library of Congress Cataloging-in-Publication Data
Bailey, Jill.
Falcons / Jill Bailey.
p. cm. -- (Secret world of--)
Summary: Provides detailed information on the physical characteristics,
evolution, various species, behavior, habitat, life cycle, and interaction with
humans of falcons, some of the world's fastest birds.
Includes bibliographical references (p.).
ISBN 0-7398-4985-9
1. Falcons--Juvenile literature. [1. Falcons. 2. Endangered species.]
I. Title. II. Series
QL696.F34 B28 2002
598.9'6--dc21

2002017770

Printed and bound in the United States
1 2 3 4 5 6 7 8 9 0 LB 06 05 04 03 02

Contents

CHAPTER 1
Built For Speed

 The Philippine falconet is the smallest bird of prey in the world. It is just 6 inches (15 cm) long, has a wingspan of 7–8 inches (18–20 cm) and weighs only 1.6 ounces (45g).

 The peregrine falcon has the widest distribution of any falcon, from the Arctic tundra to the deserts of North America, Africa, and Australia.

 The American kestrel is one of the longest-lived falcons, with a lifespan of over 12 years in the wild and 17 years in captivity.

 The largest falcon in the world is the gyrfalcon, which can measure up to 24 inches (60 cm) in length and can weigh as much as 9 pounds (4kg).

 The most numerous falcon is the Eurasian kestrel. There are probably at least 4 million pairs.

Falcons are some of the fastest birds in the world. Built for speed, many snatch their prey right out of the air, while others swoop to the ground so rapidly that their quarry does not even see them coming.

There are about 63 different kinds, or species, of falcon. They range from tiny falconets that are only a few inches long to large falcons that measure up to two feet in length. Falcons are found all over the world from the Arctic in the north to the sub-Antarctic islands in the south and from the deserts of Africa to the mountains of South America.

Falcons have highly streamlined bodies, shaped something like torpedoes. They have long wings and a long tail, which helps them to twist and turn in the air at lightning speed.

Like all birds of prey, falcons have a hooked bill for tearing at flesh, and powerful toes armed with curving claws (talons) to seize and grip their prey. Because most falcons pursue and catch their prey in midair, their toes and claws are extra-long, increasing their chances of capturing prey.

The talons are also used for defense. A falcon may tilt its body back to strike with its talons at an enemy—a serious threat to potential egg thieves. Unlike other hawks and eagles, falcons will hold food in one foot while feeding.

Patterns
Many falcons have striking barred patterns on their feathers. These markings and the distinctive shape of the bird allow identification of different species in flight.

Eyes
A falcon has extremely good eyesight. From a great height it can spot small animals moving on the ground.

Feathers
A falcon's wing feathers do not separate in flight. This distinguishes it from other birds of prey.

Wings
With long, tapering wings and a streamlined body, falcons are fast flyers, and many use their long talons to catch their prey in the air.

A falcon has long wings, quite a long tail, large eyes, and a hooked bill. This bird is hovering—the wings are beating at a steep angle and the tail feathers are spread to slow any forward or backward movement.

Most falcons appear to be drably colored, which helps camouflage them from their prey. Up close, however, many species have striking dark or light bars on their legs or tails, and the subtle shading in their plumage can be very beautiful. The laughing falcon that is native to Central and South America has a striking black face mask. In many species the males and females have very different-colored plumage.

A true falcon, the peregrine uses its long toes and talons to snatch other birds out of the air.

At the base of the beak a falcon has a patch of bare skin called a cere, which is often brightly colored. Many falcons also have a ring of colored bare skin encircling each eye, and some have colored eyelids.

There are four main groups of falcons—the true falcons, the forest falcons, the falconets and pygmy falcons, and the caracaras.

TRUE FALCONS

True falcons are open country birds with relatively long wings for fast flying. They have particularly powerful talons for seizing prey on the wing and perhaps the most acute eyesight of all the falcons. They use a variety of hunting techniques, from still hunting to low aerial pursuit, hovering and swooping, and sky-diving. True falcons are found all over the world except Antarctica, but the greatest number of species is found in Africa.

FOREST FALCONS

These falcons live in the forests of Central and South America, where they feed mainly on ground-dwelling small mammals, lizards, and insects. They have shorter,

The barred forest falcon has a very long tail. A crescent of flattened feathers below each eye funnels sound into the ears to help the bird hunt in dim light.

more rounded wings than true falcons, since long wings would be a disadvantage when flying through the trees. Their extra-long tails help them navigate between the branches; they flare out the tail and twist it to act as a rudder to help them steer. Because long aerial chases are not very practical in the dense growth of the tropical rain forest, forest falcons prefer to sit on a branch or in a bush and wait for prey to pass nearby.

FALCONETS AND PYGMY FALCONS

The smallest of all falcons, these little birds are about the size of finches and thrushes. They live in tropical and sub-tropical bush country in South America, Africa, and Southeast Asia. They hunt by darting out from a favorite perch to seize a flying insect or swooping down to take one from the ground below, then returning to their perch to eat it. The larger species attack prey as large as small lizards, mice, and small birds. The spot-winged falconet of Argentina will attack birds almost as big as itself. The local people call it "Rey de los pájaros," which means "king of the birds."

CARACARAS

Caracaras are the falcon equivalent of vultures. Named for their loud, raucous calls, they are found from the southern United States south all the way to the islands around Antarctica, including the Falkland Islands. Caracaras are large, slow, long-legged falcons with rather chunky bodies. They feed mainly on the ground by walking in search of food such as carrion (including road kills), beetles, worms, mice, lizards, and even plants. Avid scavengers, they will follow people, hoping to find cast-off food. In the Falkland Islands, the Johnny Rook (striated caracara) scavenges along the shoreline most of the year. During the breeding season, the striated caracara feeds on

The African pygmy falcon is only about 7 inches (18 cm) long. It darts out from a favorite perch to grab insects or mice moving along the ground below.

the dead young from the huge penguin and seal colonies along the coast.

Like vultures, caracaras have bare skin on their faces. This patch is often brightly colored. For example, the common caracara, which breeds as far north as Florida, has a bright orange-red face. During courtship, or when it faces a challenge to its territory, its face may flush yellow.

A young striated caracara, or Johnny Rook, pauses for a stretch while scavenging along a Falkland Island shoreline.

Instant Death

What makes falcons unique is the way they kill their prey. A special notch in the upper bill allows a falcon's beak to close between the prey's neck vertebrae (small bones) and deliver a bite that severs its neck and spinal cord, causing instant death. Only falcons have this notch. Falcons rely on surprise to catch their prey. Swooping at great speed from above or sneaking up from below, they strike the prey with their talons to knock it to the ground. The blow may even kill it outright.

I DIDN'T KNOW THAT

11

CHAPTER 2
Flight

 A stooping peregrine falcon strikes its prey in mid-air at over 150 miles per hour (240 kph), killing it instantly.

 The merlin, which is also known as the pigeon hawk, sometimes mimics the undulating flight of woodpeckers and jays to deceive its prey.

 The Australian kestrel can fly at 20 mph (32 kph). The American kestrel is faster, at 36 mph (58 kph), while the merlin can attain 45 mph (72 kph) in horizontal flight.

Their streamlined shape helps falcons reach amazing speeds in flight. A torpedo-shaped body with smooth contours provided by the flattened outer feathers offers minimum resistance to the air as the falcon hurtles through it. The bird can spread or close its tail feathers to slow down or speed up. By spreading and twisting its tail feathers it can turn at great speed—with the tail acting like the rudder of a boat.

The long tapering wings of falcons distinguish them from other birds of prey, such as hawks and eagles, and add to their speed by reducing

The gyrfalcon is the fastest falcon in level flight, even faster than a peregrine. It hunts low over the ground and may pursue its prey for miles.

A FALCON'S WING

A falcon's wing acts like an airfoil. The air passing over the upper surface of an airfoil has to travel further than the air passing over the under surface. This creates a difference in air pressure. The greater air pressure under the wing generates an upward force called lift, helping to keep the bird up in the air.

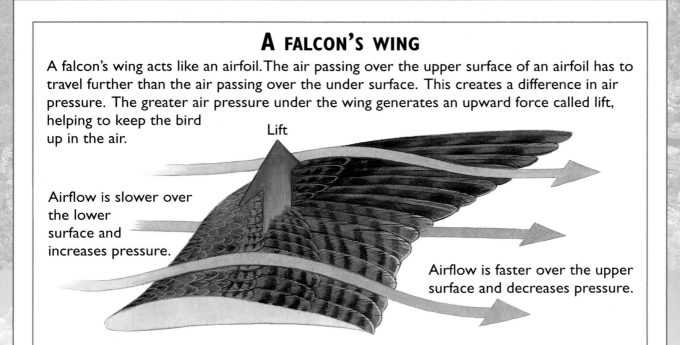

Lift

Airflow is slower over the lower surface and increases pressure.

Airflow is faster over the upper surface and decreases pressure.

drag (friction with the air) as they fly. Extremely fast flyers such as hobbies, which are native to Europe, Africa, and Asia, have especially long, tapered wings.

AIRFOILS

In flight the falcon's wing forms an airfoil—a slightly arched structure, like the wing of an airplane. Air rushing over the arched upper surface exerts less pressure than the air passing across the flatter lower surface. The greater pressure on the underside of the wing creates an upward force, called lift, which enables the bird to rise and stay up in the air. Even individual feathers are shaped like airfoils.

For short distances and at low altitudes falcons flap their wings to fly. Flapping flight requires a lot of energy, but produces speed. Forest-dwelling falcons rely on flapping flight and can put on a great burst of speed to catch their prey. The large gyrfalcon can maintain fast flapping flight over long distances across the open tundra. Although the peregrine falcon is one of the fastest birds, in level flight it is easily outdistanced by many types of birds, including racer pigeons. It achieves its great speeds—and catches its prey—by swooping or diving from great heights. These dives are called "stoops."

The Secret of Speed

In the 1940s the British Navy analyzed film of a peregrine stoop and estimated its top speed at 273 miles per hour (439 kph). More recent research suggests 175 mph (282 kph) as a more likely top speed, but this is still impressive. How does it do it? The peregrine folds its wings and dives steeply down head first, forming a streamlined bullet-shape that offers very little resistance to the air as it plummets toward the earth. Even though it slows as it reaches its quarry, the peregrine may still strike its prey at 100 mph (160 kph), enough to kill most birds outright.

SOARING

Like many birds, falcons can glide through the air by partly spreading their wings and tail and holding them steady. As they glide, they drift slowly downward. By closing their wings more, they descend at an even steeper angle. The peregrine closes its wings almost completely to plummet down onto its prey.

Land heats up faster than air. When sunlight warms the land, the air closest to the ground becomes warmer than the air above. Warm air is less dense than cold air, so the warm air rises, forming a rising current of air called a thermal. Birds can make use of thermals to rise to great heights, spreading their wings and tails as if gliding and riding the thermal around and around and up. When they want to travel forward they first reach a good height, then glide slowly away at a gentle angle. When they need to gain more height again, they find the next thermal.

HOVERING

Some falcons, such as the kestrels, do most of their hunting by hovering above the ground, then swooping down the moment they spot prey moving below. The bird partly spreads its tail and bends it down at a steep angle, at the same time beating its wings at a steep angle, generating lift on both the upstroke and the downstroke. Any forward propulsion generated by the downstroke is exactly cancelled out by the upstroke, so the bird remains in the same place. Most kestrels are native to Europe. The only kind found in the United States is commonly known as the sparrow hawk.

IDENTIFYING FALCONS IN FLIGHT

As well as their tapered wings, falcons can be distinguished from other birds of prey because their wings do not have spread "fingers" of feathers at the tip. Their wings have a smooth outline. Hovering falcons, such as kestrels, usually have relatively long tails, as do forest falcons.

Most field guides to birds of prey give pictures of the birds viewed in flight from both above and below to aid in identification of both species and sex. The overall size of the bird and the habitat in which it is seen are also significant.

The pattern of dark and light colors and banding on the breast, the undersides of the wings, and the tail are important guides in identifying falcon species. This is a lanner falcon.

CHAPTER 3
Sight and Hearing

 By turning its head, a falcon can survey its surroundings over an angle of 340 degrees—almost a full circle.

 Even while hovering so high that a human cannot see it, a falcon is able to spot a mouse on the ground.

 Kestrels derive their name from the French word *crecerelle* (a noisy bell) or *crecelle* (to ring).

 Unlike other falcons, the forest falcon relies on its exceptionally good hearing to catch its prey, in the semi-dark forests in which it lives.

Most falcons rely mainly on sight to detect and capture their prey. Like other birds of prey, falcons have exceptionally large eyes for their size—so large that they almost fill the eye socket and cannot move much. Falcons make up for this by having a very

A "bird's-eye view" of a landscape from the air. A falcon flying at this height could spot a small animal such as a mouse moving on the ground below.

This prairie falcon's eyes take up such a large proportion of the space in its skull that there is no room for muscles to move them; the falcon has an extremely flexible neck instead.

flexible neck, so they can swivel their head around to look to the side or even behind them. The eyes face directly forward, which gives these birds their very direct, penetrating stare. The fields of view of the two eyes overlap, so they have good binocular vision.

This allows them to accurately judge distance and speed—a great advantage in the chase.

The human eye has a pit, called the fovea, at the back in which the light-receiving cells are highly concentrated, giving very acute vision. Birds of prey have even sharper sight because the light-sensitive cells in their eyes are even more densely packed. They have two foveas, one providing acute vision straight ahead, and the other providing detailed sideways vision. Their eyes are often proportionally larger than ours, so the image that enters the eye is bigger.

HEARING

Falcons use calls to communicate with each other. Adult falcons use a range of whistles, screams, yelps, yaps, croaks, barks, cackles, and mews, according to the species and the situation. There are different calls for threats, courtship, bringing food to the nest, or proclaiming a breeding territory. Forest falcons use calls to communicate in dense vegetation, usually either yapping noises or more songbird-like calls. Young falcons make soft calls to get their parents' attention, and louder ones when begging for food. Female falcons use similar calls to persuade the males to bring them food.

A young striated caracara calls to its parent, begging for food. Adults can recognize their young by their calls.

The Third Eyelid

Falcons, like many birds, have a third eyelid, a translucent membrane that they can draw from back to front across the eye to protect it while in flight, seizing prey, or feeding their young. This extra eyelid, called the nictitating membrane, also helps keep their eyes moist.

I DIDN'T KNOW THAT !

SOUND FUNNELS

Forest falcons, which live in dense vegetation, have well-developed ears and probably rely on hearing to catch prey in dim light. They hunt mainly around dusk and dawn, as do such species as the bat falcon and hobby, which sometimes hunt bats by moonlight.

These species have a ruff of small, stiff feathers around each of their ears. The ruff funnels sound into the ear, in much the same way that the huge cheek-like discs of feathers on an owl's face do. Together with extra large ear openings, this provides for a very acute sense of hearing—essential for hunting in dim light.

The flattened feathers on a forest falcon's face funnel sound into its ears.

CHAPTER 4
Hunting Techniques

Famed for their abilities as hunters, falcons rely on speed and surprise to capture prey that is often almost as big as they are. Depending on the species of the falcon and the landscape it is hunting in, the falcon may chase its prey across the sky, swoop down on it from a perch, or even run after it on foot. Kestrels hover above the ground while looking for prey.

Like owls, falcons cough up pellets of undigested material, such as fur, feathers, insect skeletons, beetle

The American kestrel, or sparrow hawk, needs to eat 21 percent of its body weight in food each day.

Falcons need more food in winter than in summer, as they use up energy keeping warm. The peregrine falcon consumes 11.5 percent of its body weight each day in winter, but only 1 percent in warm weather.

A gyrfalcon pair needs a territory of up to 400 square miles (1030 sq km) to provide it with enough food, whereas a pair of pygmy falcons needs only 0.4 sq miles (1 sq km).

The American red-throated caracara feeds mainly on wasp larvae, while the barred kestrel specializes in eating chameleons.

Lesser kestrels will steal food from the nests of their neighbors.

Falcons, such as this peregrine, regularly pluck the larger feathers from their prey while sitting on a favorite perch. Feathers on the ground below provide clues to the falcon's recent diet.

wing-cases, and so on. By analyzing the pellets, scientists can find out what the bird has been eating.

FEEDING TERRITORIES

Most falcons defend an area of land, their "home range," against other falcons of the same species. The size of this territory reflects the area of land needed to provide sufficient food for the bird or for a pair of birds. During the breeding season, the birds will defend a larger "breeding territory" that can provide enough food for themselves and their growing family.

Birds such as the gyrfalcon, which hunt in areas with low numbers of prey, may have very large territories. The peregrine falcon needs a home range of only 17 square miles (44 sq km) in country that is rich in prey, but on the bleak Scottish moorlands its territory may cover 40 square miles (100 sq km).

A falcon will often tolerate birds of other species in its territory, providing they do not compete directly for the same food resources. During the breeding season, however, it may be aggressive toward all birds. Prairie

An American kestrel hides its prey, in this case an insect, in a hollow tree. It will return to its larder when food is scarce.

falcons will drive off peregrine falcons, which may compete for the same prey, but they will tolerate ravens, even though ravens feed on bird eggs. Small falcons such as kestrels and merlins will not hesitate to attack larger birds of prey that intrude on their territory.

American kestrels and some other falcons regularly store food in caches such as hollow trees, rock crevices, and even the switchboxes of telegraph poles. When prey is plentiful, they stock these larders.

STILL HUNTING

Falconets and pygmy falcons are lazy hunters. These little birds hunt rather like flycatchers, waiting on a favorite perch for insects to pass within reach, then making a quick dash to capture them in the air or on the ground. This method is called "still hunting."

The forest falcons of Central and South America use a similar "dive and dash" technique, lying in wait hidden on a leafy branch, then dashing out and pursuing their prey through the lower canopy of the rain forest. One type of forest falcon, the laughing falcon (named for its laughing cries), specializes in catching snakes. It swallows small snakes whole but bites off the heads of larger ones before eating them.

A peregrine falcon swoops toward the ground, its talons spread wide to seize its prey, which is hidden behind the rock.

HOVERING AND DIVING

Where prey is plentiful, most falcons "still hunt." From a high perch such as a telegraph wire or even the ledge of a building, they use their acute vision to spot prey long before the prey spots them.

Kestrels use an even higher vantage point. While hovering in one spot hundreds of feet above the ground, they can spot the tiniest movement of a mouse, vole, or even a beetle. A rapid dive usually surprises the prey, though some small mammals have good enough eyesight to spot the danger just in time.

THE AERIAL CHASE

The masters of the aerial chase are the bat falcon and the hobby. The bat falcon of South and Central America will catch almost anything that flies—birds, bats, and insects, including large dragonflies. It frequents open areas such as the edges of forests and clearings, rivers, roads, and fields. Launching its attack from a high perch, it approaches its prey rapidly from behind, dropping down below it to make an unexpected strike from below, its legs and feet stretched out. Using bushes and low branches for cover as it approaches, it seldom needs to hunt far from its perch.

Hobbies, which live in Europe, Africa, Asia, Australia, and New Zealand, are capable of catching fast-flying birds such as swallows and swifts. Their usual technique is to pursue the birds from below rather than above, then strike upward. Birds usually spot another bird approaching from above them, but are less aware of approaches from behind and below. When hunting birds such as gulls, the gyrfalcon sometimes chases them high into the air and forces them to stay aloft until they tire and have to seek cover.

The hobby is a master of the aerial chase, rushing up from below to snatch fast-flying birds such as swallows and martins out of the air.

GROUND PURSUIT

A few falcons, especially large falcons such as the gyrfalcon and the North American prairie falcon, chase their prey at low altitudes and knock it to the ground. The gyrfalcon lives in the wide open spaces of Arctic North America, Europe, and Asia and hunts mainly ptarmigan, ground squirrels, lemmings, and sometimes ducks. Once it spots a potential meal, it may wait until the prey is temporarily out of sight before starting its pursuit, so that it cannot be seen. It flies low and very fast, choosing a flight path that allows it to hide behind rocks or bushes. The gyrfalcon can chase prey for several miles.

The lanner falcon of southern Europe, Africa, and Asia hunts in a similar way, and is also said to be able to surprise a rat standing by its own burrow. The saker falcon of the grassy plains of Asia, another high-speed falcon, also hunts close to the ground for mice, voles, and hamsters, but at times it may hover instead, like a giant kestrel.

The merlin is one of the fastest birds in the world in level flight. It chases its prey from behind, sometimes rising above it at the last instant before swooping. It tends to hunt close to the ground, usually less than a meter above. The gray falcon of the deserts of Australia may hunt close to the ground like a merlin, chasing birds, lizards, insects, and young rabbits, but it can also chase flying insects high in the air like a hobby.

Highly prized by falconers, the lanner falcon often hunts with its mate. One bird flushes the prey from its hiding place into the path of its partner, a tactic so successful that it can even catch other birds of prey.

Mantling

When a falcon lands its newly killed prey on the ground or brings it back to the nest, it hunches over it, wings spread and eyes glaring. This is called mantling. Making the falcon look larger and fiercer than it really is, this is a threat display intended to deter any other creature from stealing its prey. It is instinctive behavior: even young falcons mantle over morsels brought to them by their parents.

SCARE TACTICS

The black falcon of Australia, which tends to launch attacks from quite a low altitude, does not abandon its pursuit easily. It screams loudly as it chases its prey. Even if the prey takes cover in a tree or bush, it will continue to dive at it, screaming and hoping to frighten it into leaving its shelter.

WORKING TOGETHER

Most falcons hunt alone or with their mate. When a pair hunt together, one bird often flies ahead to flush out the prey, while the other follows behind to attack. Or they may both approach the same prey but from different angles, confusing it and leaving it little opportunity to escape.

Some falcons regularly hunt in groups. Where food is scarce, many pairs of eyes have a better chance of finding it. Lesser kestrels, from Africa, sometimes hunt in small parties. They fly over a patch of ground, then hover for a closer look. If they do not spot prey they move on and hover over a different place. Several other falcon species, such as Eurasian hobbies, live in flocks outside the breeding season but separate into pairs to breed.

CHAPTER 5
Reproduction

Falcons return again and again to favorite nesting sites, often for generations. Some peregrine falcon nesting sites in England have been in use since at least the 13th century.

The female American kestrel may produce more than half of her body weight in eggs in a single week—a good reason why feeding is part of a falcon's courtship ritual.

Eleonora's falcons breed on islands in the Mediterranean Sea. They feed their chicks on songbirds that migrate south across the Mediterranean to spend winter in Africa.

African pygmy falcons nest inside the communal nests of buffalo weavers, birds much smaller than themselves.

Most falcons do not make nests, but many species use the nests of other birds, especially the abandoned nests of crows and ravens. Forest falcons will lay their eggs in natural tree hollows. Falcons that live in open areas, such as the prairie, lanner, and saker falcons, use their feet to make a shallow scrape in the ground or on a cliff ledge—just sufficient to prevent the eggs from

This African pygmy falcon has made its home inside the communal nest of a colony of weaver birds. At other times of year it would kill and eat the weavers, but they seem quite content to let it live among them.

A Eurasian kestrel nests in a flower box on a windowsill in an Israeli town, a soft substitute for a wild cliff.

rolling off or away. Kestrels will nest in hay barns and in artificial nestboxes. Caracaras nest on the ground, where they make shallow nests of twigs or grasses, sometimes lining them with sheep's wool.

The area a pair of falcons needs to supply enough food for its young (its breeding territory) may differ from its usual territory, and falcons become much more sensitive to intruders in their territories during the breeding seasons. Even in species that nest in large groups, such as Eleonora's falcon, the nests are spaced out, and birds returning with food follow very specific flight paths that avoid the air over their neighbors' nests. Falcons often use aerial displays accompanied by special cries to proclaim their breeding territories.

COURTSHIP DISPLAYS

Many falcons use spectacular aerial displays when courting. These probably help the prospective partners to judge each other's fitness. Once they have paired up, falcons often remain faithful to their mates for life. Even species that form large flocks outside the breeding season and migrate long distances usually return to the same mate next season.

Usually, the male puts on a display for the female. The male American kestrel, for instance, flies overhead with his wingtips quivering, calling to the female, and from time to time makes dramatic dives toward her. The lanner falcon will pursue a mate through the air; once they have accepted each other, they will soar and dive through the sky together. Falcons that stay together throughout the year, such as the peregrine, may conduct a kind of year-round aerial display, consisting of mock chases and plunges. When the two partners are close to each other, they perform a bowing ritual, calling to each other softly.

Courtship usually also involves the male bringing food to the female. She may solicit food from him by adopting the crouching position and begging calls of a young falcon. The amount of food she is given also helps her to decide whether her prospective mate is a good hunter and can provide for the family.

In most falcons, the female is considerably larger than the male. The American kestrel female (right) is no exception.

28

DIFFERENT ROLES

Male and female falcons play different roles in bringing up their family. The female incubates the eggs, with the male taking over for short periods while she feeds. Females develop a "brood patch" in the breeding season, an area of bare skin on their belly where the eggs can come into direct contact with their warm skin.

Once the young have hatched, the male continues to bring food for his mate and his offspring, while the female stays to keep them warm, or shade them from the sun, and defend them from intruders. Eventually the young require so much food that the mother has to start hunting again.

THE BIRTH OF A FALCON

The eggs of falcons and caracaras are a round oval shape, usually reddish or buffish brown in color, and often speckled. The inside of the shell is ocher-colored. The female lays an egg every two or three days until the clutch is complete. Falcons lay three to seven eggs at a time, with small falcons laying more eggs than larger ones. Incubation may last for

A clutch of merlin eggs. Falcon eggs are usually reddish or buff in color and slightly tapered at one end, to keep them from rolling around.

three weeks for small species and up to five weeks for larger falcons.

The chicks start calling to their mother before they hatch. Hatching can be a difficult business. Each chick has extra-strong neck muscles and a tooth-like projection ("egg tooth") on the tip of its bill to help it break through the egg. Even so, it can take more than a day to escape. The egg tooth falls off later. Young falcons are often referred to as eyasses. When first hatched, their eyes are only partly open, and they are covered in warm, fluffy down. They can barely lift up their head to be fed.

GROWING UP

All the young falcons get a fairly equal share of food. After about a week they develop a second coat of down, which is much thicker. Now they look somewhat comical and cuddly—a ball of fluff with big, glaring, fierce eyes, supported on huge feet.

By the time they begin to grow true feathers, the eyasses are eating almost as much as an adult. The female carefully tears off small pieces to feed them. As they grow, she gives them larger pieces, until

These brown falcon nestlings still have downy, fluffy fur among their more adult feathers, making them look much plumper than they really are.

Imprinting

Falcon chicks learn to recognize the animal that feeds and cares for them as a member of their own species. This is called imprinting. A young falcon that is fed by a human, for example, may come to identify that person as its parent. As it grows older, the falcon may identify other humans as "birds" like itself and seek to court them as a mate. That is why humans who raise falcons wear a puppet-like glove that resembles the head of an adult falcon of the right species when feeding them.

Before these young birds raised by humans can be released into the wild, they have to learn to hunt. They are taken to a high place, like a tower, and kept in a cage where they can see the land around them. Once they become used to this, they are allowed to fly free, and they are given food at the tower until they have learned to hunt for themselves. This may take several months, but eventually they will go off on their own.

I DIDN'T KNOW THAT

eventually they are left to deal with the carcass themselves.

Small falcons may be ready to leave the nest, or "fledge," after just four weeks, but the young of larger species, such as the lanner and gyrfalcons, may stay in the nest for up to seven weeks. As they near the time to leave, the eyasses spend more and more time at the edge of the nest or on nearby branches, flapping their wings and making little jumps into the air.

LEARNING NEW SKILLS

Young falcons have a lot to learn as they prepare to leave their parents. Most important of all, they have to learn to catch their own prey. As they grow bigger, their parents may start to bring home live prey, usually small animals such as mice, for them to learn to kill. They may teach their young hunting skills by dropping live prey in the air for them to hunt.

While still in the nest, young falcons may play with the prey. They will also grab and squeeze objects in the nest, such as stones or twigs, practicing the grip that they will eventually use on live prey. Later, they learn other skills by engaging in mock fights with each other in the air.

A peregrine falcon daintily plucks small morsels of food from its catch to feed its young chicks.

CHAPTER 6
Migration

 One-fourth of all birds of prey migrate between breeding season and winter or dry season feeding areas each year.

 Red-footed falcons migrate all the way from eastern Siberia and China to southern Africa and back.

 Eleonora's falcons nest around Mediterranean coasts, feeding their young on migrating songbirds. They spend winter in Madagascar, where they eat mainly insects.

 At Eilat in Israel and at the Panama Canal, over 1,000,000 birds of prey may pass overhead in a single season.

MAIN MIGRATION ROUTES

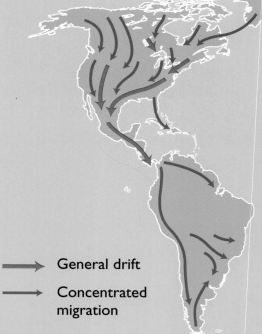

→ General drift

→ Concentrated migration

Most migration takes place along specific routes or "flyways," where the birds can take advantage of favorable winds and where there are places to stop and hunt.

Many species of falcon move from place to place at different times of the year. When this pattern of movement is consistent over a number of years, it is called migration. The birds move to areas where prey is more abundant to breed and rear

The red-footed falcon is one of the few falcons to migrate over water. It crosses the Indian Ocean from India to southeast Africa and back each year.

In the Americas, there are major flyways along the Pacific and Atlantic coasts, while other flyways stretch from the Arctic, Russia, and Scandinavia across Europe to the west and east coasts of Africa.

SEASONED TRAVELERS

The real long-distance travelers are the red-footed falcons, Amur falcons, and lesser kestrels, some of which migrate from India to East Africa. The Eurasian hobby migrates from northern Europe and Russia to southern Africa and southern Asia. Other falcons make shorter migrations: the gyrfalcon and peregrine will fly as far as 430 miles (688 km) over the Labrador Sea from Greenland to Labrador, while the merlin journeys 500 miles (800 km) from Iceland across the Atlantic Ocean to Great Britain and Ireland.

their young. Some take advantage of the abundance of prey found only in summer in regions such as the Arctic tundra or the grasslands of Asia and North America. In desert regions, many falcons breed during the rainy season, traveling north to the grasslands when the rain comes. Others migrate away from areas that have sufficient prey in order to avoid competing with other species that are rearing families at the same time.

These ocean travelers are the exception. Generally, falcons do not like to fly long distances over water. There is nowhere to rest, and there are no thermals to help them on their way. Where they can, some falcons will island-hop. Most falcons prefer to travel along the coast, converging at the mouths of gulfs and narrow straits of water. The birds do not even like crossing large bays, so they stream along the shores instead.

TIME TO GO

A falcon's urge to migrate is instinctive. The instinct to migrate is inherited, but the specific day on which migration occurs in a year is triggered by factors such as the length of the day and the weather. A change in the amount of daylight signals the approaching change of seasons. Then, changes are triggered in the bird's internal chemistry, such as the storage of fat to provide energy for the long flight. Once the daylight has triggered these changes, the birds usually wait for favorable wind directions to help them on their way.

Most falcons are thought to migrate by day, but peregrines have been detected migrating at night. By day they use the position of the sun to judge their direction. They may not travel on wet, cloudy days. Some birds are thought to use the stars to navigate at night, but it is not known if falcons do so.

With its large, powerful wings, the gyrfalcon has no problem migrating long distances.

We know that pigeons are guided by the earth's magnetic field. Other guideposts along flyways are mountains and other natural landmarks. Birds can detect low frequency sound given off by winds rising over hills or sweeping into valleys and by waves along the coast. Such sounds, too low for the human ear to hear, can travel for hundreds of miles.

NOMADS

Many falcons that do not migrate annually nevertheless move from one area to another at different times of the year. Where local food sources vary according to the season, where insect life flourishes after sporadic rains, or where prey becomes scarce for any reason, falcons may travel considerable distances in search of food. When such journeys are not made regularly to or from a breeding area, they are referred to as nomadic movements rather than migration.

A Safe Refuge

The great concentration of birds along migration flyways have always attracted human hunters. The world's first refuge for migrating birds of prey was created in 1934 in the Appalachian Mountains of the eastern United States. A group of concerned conservationists led by Rosalie Edge purchased the top of Hawk Mountain to create a sanctuary for hawks, falcons, eagles, and other birds. The sanctuary also attracted birdwatchers and tourist revenue. By the early 1990s it was receiving over 50,000 visitors a year from all over the world.

I DIDN'T KNOW THAT

CHAPTER 7
Falconry

 Falconry is thought to have begun at least 4,000 years ago in Asia or the Middle East.

 In the Middle Ages, falconry was so popular that people took their falcons to church with them.

 The German king Frederick II of Hohenstaufen, who ruled the Holy Roman Empire from 1212 to 1250, is regarded as one of the greatest falconers who ever lived. His book on falconry is still consulted today.

 Some airfields use falcons to scare other birds away from the aircraft.

 There are about 20,000 falconers in the world today.

▶ A falconer grasps the leather jesses as his peregrine falcon waits patiently on his gauntlet for the command to hunt.

Falconry is the art of training falcons and other birds of prey to hunt birds or small mammals. The human who trains these birds is called a falconer. The birds are trained to sit on the falconer's arm, on a special long, thick, leather glove called a gauntlet. At a command from the falconer, the bird takes to the air to pursue its prey. It then brings the dead birds or mammals back to the falconer, who rewards it with food.

Falconry dates back thousands of years. There are descriptions of hunting with falcons in Chinese writings from the 7th century B.C. One of the most famous

VM ETSVI MILITES :EQVI TANT: AD BOS

One of the earliest pictures of falconry, the Bayeux Tapestry dates to the 11th century, when soldiers used to take their falcons to war with them.

portrayals is part of the Bayeux Tapestry, which was created to celebrate the Norman conquest of Britain of 1066. In the Middle Ages, falconry was a popular sport in many countries. Soldiers took falcons with them to war, taking time out from the fighting to fly them. Falconry used to be the most efficient way of catching wild birds.

THE SPORT OF KINGS

From the Middle East to Europe, falconry was for centuries the sport of kings and nobility. In some countries, a peasant could be executed for taking a wild falcon from its nest.

The Boke [Book] of St. Albans, written by an abbess in the 15th century, outlines who was allowed to fly which birds. Emperors could fly golden eagles or gyrfalcons; princes, a female peregrine; knights, a lanner falcon; noblewomen, the smaller merlin; yeomen and the land-owning upper classes, the northern goshawk; priests, a female Eurasian sparrowhawk; and knaves, servants, and children, a Eurasian kestrel.

Falconers show off their birds at a falcon market in Riyadh, Saudi Arabia. Falconry is a very popular pastime in the Middle East and Asia.

prey to the ground, often killing it outright. For falconers, this is the most exciting moment of the chase.

Until the falcon is ready to hunt, the falconer places a soft, leather hood over the bird's head. This keeps it from becoming distracted and flying off after other prey.

Thin strips of leather called "jesses" are looped around the falcon's legs. The falconer can hold these while the bird is on his wrist, and they can be looped around its perch when the falcon is back home. When the falcon is flying free, the jesses stream out behind it.

TRAINING FALCONS

Taming and training a falcon takes a long time and a lot of patience. The bird must learn to

HUNTING WITH FALCONS

Today's falconers often team their falcons with a dog. The dog runs on ahead, sniffing for birds hidden in the vegetation. When it picks up a scent, it "points," freezing with its nose pointing in the direction of the scent. Sometimes the prey, too, freezes and will often only leave its hiding place at the very last moment. The falconer now sets the bird loose. It flies up from his or her fist, spiraling overhead to reach a suitable height for a stoop. Then it waits for the falconer to "put up," or startle, the prey. The falcon stoops and knocks the trust the falconer, and the falconer must learn to communicate with the bird.

First the young bird has to learn to be at ease on the falconer's wrist, perched on his or her gauntlet. The falconer will feed the bird frequently with tidbits to reward good behavior or simply to calm it if it is nervous. Once the falcon gets used to the falconer, the lessons begin.

The next stage is called "calling off." The bird is allowed to fly some distance away, prevented from escaping by a light cord (called a "creance") around its legs. Then it is tempted back to the fist by more food. Gradually the bird is allowed to fly farther away, until eventually it no longer needs to be held by the cord. Now the falconer uses a lure—a chunk of rabbit fur attached to a cord— to teach the bird to spot and catch a body in motion. The falconer whirls the lure around, encouraging the falcon to stoop at it. It if makes a successful stoop, it gets fed some more. Once the falcon has mastered this test, it is ready for its first real hunt.

Falcons as Gods

Falcons have played key roles in legends, myths, and religions for thousands of years. In ancient Egyptian hieroglyphics, the symbol of a falcon was used to represent a king. The god Horus, who took the form of a falcon, was a very important deity. Some 800,000 mummified falcons, mostly kestrels, were found in chambers under some of the Egyptian temples.

CHAPTER 8
Threats and Conservation

 Over 20 species of falcons are now bred in captivity, and several threatened species have been reestablished in the wild from captive-bred stock.

 Between 1837 and 1840, on a single estate at Glengarry in Scotland, a total of 1,392 birds of prey were killed by hunters: 98 peregrines, 78 merlins, 462 kestrels, 285 buzzards, 3 honey-buzzards, 15 golden eagles, 27 white-tailed eagles, 18 ospreys, 63 northern goshawks, 275 red kites, and 68 harriers.

The only species of falcon known to become extinct in the last three centuries is the Guadalupe caracara, which was once found only on the tiny island of Guadalupe off the coast of Baja California.

For much of the 19th and 20th centuries, wild falcons have been threatened by humans. On country estates where pheasants and grouse were reared to be shot for sport, birds of prey were regarded as enemies by gamekeepers and shot indiscriminately. Birds of prey were also killed accidentally by poisoned bait intended for foxes, jackals, and other vermin. Today, farmers are coming to realize the valuable service these birds provide as

The New Zealand bush falcon is found only in beech forests in a small area of New Zealand, and has probably never lived anywhere else.

Almost Extinct

The Mauritius kestrel is found only on the island of Mauritius in the Indian Ocean. By 1974 it was virtually extinct, with only six birds known to be living. Its decline was due partly to the pesticide DDT, but also to the introduction of macaque monkeys to Mauritius. These monkeys took eggs and young birds from their nests in the trees. Finally, some birds were taken from the wild for captive breeding. Then some of the remaining birds began to nest on cliffs instead of trees. Their offspring adopted the same habit. Other kestrels took to artificial nesting boxes. By the end of the 20th century, Mauritius was home to some 200 kestrels, probably close to the maximum number of birds the island could support.

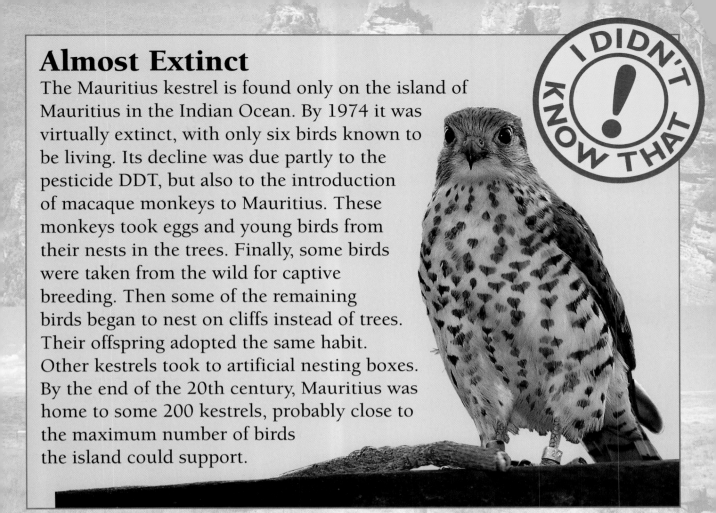

natural enemies of mice, rats, rabbits, and other pests. Public opinion in favor of conservation has led to the passage of bird protection laws in many countries. In some places, it is illegal even to photograph a falcon at its nest site.

Such legislation has helped to reduce the numbers shot as pests or taken from the wild for private collections or falconry. The collection of falcon eggs is also prohibited. Even so, falcons are still losing their habitats to other human activities. As the human population increases and expands its living space, forests are felled, wetlands are drained, grasslands are burned, and huge stretches of country are given over to cities and towns. The result is massive loss of habitat for falcons and the animals they prey on. Today this is a particularly great threat to the forest falcons of Central and South America.

POISONED

After World War II, a chemical known as DDT became widely used all over the world as a pesticide, both on agricultural land and to kill mosquitoes and their larvae in swamps and waterways. This insecticide also proved poisonous to small insect-eating animals and to the birds that fed on them. In the United States, for example, the peregrine falcon was almost wiped out; by the mid-1960s there was not a single nesting pair east of the Mississippi River.

ENDANGERED

A number of species of falcons are considered at risk of extinction today. Many countries have signed an agreement called CITES (the Convention on International Trade in Endangered Species) that outlaws trade in endangered animals or in products made from them. Under CITES, falcons worldwide may be traded only under special license.

It is becoming much easier to detect birds that have been stolen or reared from stolen eggs. Even if the thief produces false papers for the falcon, genetic tests will soon prove whether it has captive-bred parents or not.

SUCCESS STORIES

Some threatened falcons have been saved by special captive-breeding techniques. Most falcons will lay a second clutch, or group, of eggs if anything happens to the first one before the eggs hatch. Breeders can remove the first clutch from the

A kestrel nesting box on the back of a highway sign in Idaho. These extra nesting sites have helped kestrel numbers to increase.

A female American kestrel incubates her eggs in the shelter of a nest box.

birds and place the eggs with captive foster parents, or rear the young by hand in incubators. Then the wild birds will go on to produce another brood of their own. Captive breeding has helped to save the Mauritius kestrel, taita falcon, and peregrine.

Some species can be helped by providing more nest sites, especially nest boxes. The American kestrel will use boxes. In the Midwest, these are attached to the back of interstate highway signs. It is also possible to make artificial cavities in cliffs for prairie and peregrine falcons to use as nest sites.

FALCONS IN CITIES

The spread of towns and cities has not been all bad news for falcons. Some have adapted to make use of the extra nest sites offered by ledges on high-rise buildings. Kestrels and peregrines regularly nest in cities. Hobbies find a plentiful supply of swallows and martins, which nest under the eaves of houses and sheds. City lights attract moths, providing large concentrations of easy food. Falcons will also snatch birds from garden bird-feeders.

While some people may be distressed by the sight of a falcon seizing a bird from a garden bird-feeder, falcons should be welcome arrivals to our towns and cities. They provide a valuable service by killing mice and other pests and are a wonderful symbol of the wild amid the dull concrete of urban life.

Glossary

BREEDING TERRITORY – an area defended by one or more animals against others of the same species during the breeding season. The breeding territory is often larger than the home range, since it must be of a size necessary to feed a growing family. It may even be in a different area of the home range, in a location where suitable food is more abundant.

CAPTIVE BREEDING – the breeding of animals in captivity in order to save the species, usually in the hope of raising sufficient young to return some to the wild.

CARRION – the flesh of dead animals.

CERE – a fleshy, featherless area at the base of the upper beak in some birds. It is often a different color than the rest of the face.

FALCONER – a person who trains and hunts with falcons and other birds of prey.

FALCONET – a small falcon from South America or South Asia, usually with striking black and white plumage.

FALCONRY – the keeping and training of falcons and other birds of prey for use in hunting.

HOME RANGE – an area defended by an animal or group of animals all year-round against other members of the same species.

IMPRINTING – the process by which young birds recognize their parents and acquire a knowledge of their species. Imprinting takes place at a particular stage of development, and cannot be reversed. Captive birds may imprint on their human keepers if care is not taken to prevent them being seen.

LIFT – an upward force that opposes the downward pull of gravity.

MANTLING – threatening display made by a falcon over freshly killed prey, intended to deter other animals from stealing the kill.

MIGRATION – regular movement from one region or habitat to another, often according to the seasons.

NOMADISM – the habit of moving from place to place in search of food.

SCAVENGER – an animal that feeds on dead meat or dead plant material.

STREAMLINED – shaped to offer very little resistance to air or water when moving through it.

TALON – a powerful curved claw belonging to a bird of prey and used to grip the prey.

THERMAL – an upward current of air formed when warm air rises, often used by birds, gliders, and hot air balloons to gain height.

Further Reading

Arnold, Caroline. *Saving the Peregrine Falcon*. Minneapolis: Lerner, 1990.

Kops, Deborah. *Falcons*. Woodbridge, CT: Blackbirch Press, 2000.

Olsen, Penny. *Falcons and Hawks*. New York: Facts on File, 1994.

Priebe, Mac. *The Peregrine Falcon: Endangered No More*. Norwalk, CT: Mindfull Publishing, 2000.

Acknowledgments
Ardea: page 9; **Bruce Coleman**: page 8 (Hans Reinhard), 10, 18 (Dr. Hermann Brehm), 11 (Allan G. Potts), 20 (Hans Reinhard), 24 (Sarah Cook), 25 (Kim Taylor), 36, 39 (Staffan Widstrand), 38 (Erik Bjurstrom); **NHPA**: page 12 (Gerard Lacz), 14 (Bill Coster), 15, 23, (Stephen Dalton), 16/17 (David Woodfall), 26 (Nigel J. Dennis), 28, 32 (Mike Lane), 30 (Dave Watts), 37 (G. I. Barnard), 43 (Stephen Krasemann), Cover (Stephen Dalton); **Oxford Scientific Films**: page 17 (Tom Ulrich), 21 (Daniel J. Cox), 22 (Alan & Sandy Carey), 27 (Waina Cheng), 29 (Dennis Green), 31 (Richard & Julia Kemp), 34 (Michael W. Richards) 40 (Tui de Roy), 41 (Paul Kay), 42 (Richard Day); All background images © Steck-Vaughn Collection (Corbis Royalty Free, Getty Royalty Free, and StockBYTE).

Index

Numbers in *italic* indicate pictures